– THE GREAT –
BEAR BRIGADE

SUPER SWEET SURPRISE

Illustrated by:
Javier Gimenez Ratti

Written By:
Jason Kutasi

The Great Bear Brigade has lots of stories to share.
   Once you read their adventures then you'll be aware,
Of life lessons to learn and how to take care.
   They will help you live smart and always beware!

Today is your mom's birthday,
and you need a gift...

A cake would
be perfect,
and friends make
the work swift.

But while stirring the mixture,
your minds starts to drift...

The batter makes a mess,
and your mom will be miffed.

So if you're baking a cake,
and it begins to go wrong…

The cake is over-cooked,
and the burnt smell is strong...

Just hold onto your breath,
they'll arrive before long.

And get ready to sing,
a Happy Birthday Song.

Believe it or not,

some bears like to bake...

Their skills can help you,
prevent a mistake.

If you don't make a mess,
mom can enjoy her cake...

You made it to please her,
for goodness sake!

Take the bear's advice,
they hope you will listen...

Don't be afraid to ask,
people love to pitch in...

And before you know it,
it's a cake you'll be dishin'!

The Great Bear Brigade is simply the best.
When they sense you're in trouble, they'll never rest,
And all of their skills will be put to the test.
They're happy to help, and they do it with zest!

When you have a problem that leaves you perplexed,
The bears have the answers, so you won't be vexed.
You'll be flipping the pages and reading the text,
Follow their adventures to see what comes next.

Pay special attention as the stories unfold,
These Bear Brigade adventures need to be told.